WINGO PERSEUS

Airport

Wingo Perseus has traveled extensively in the footsteps of his father, a WWII flyer. His favorite airport is City in London, most dreaded is Frankfurt, and he misses the charm of the old Delta Marine Terminal at LaGuardia. Not the best flyer himself, Wingo now lives and works as a writer outside Boston. *Airport* is Wingo Perseus' second book.

GEMMA
Open Door

First published by GemmaMedia in 2011.

GemmaMedia
230 Commercial Street
Boston, MA 02109 USA

www.gemmamedia.com

Printed in the United States of America

15   14   13   12   11   1   2   3   4   5

978-1-934848-52-4

Library of Congress Cataloging-in-Publication Data

Cover by Night & Day Design

Inspired by the Irish series of books designed for adult literacy, Gemma Open Door Foundation provides fresh stories, new ideas and essential resources for young people and adults as they embrace the power of reading and the written word.

Brian Bouldrey
North American Series Editor

GEMMA
Open Door

for Patrick

CONTENTS

ONE

Check In

The camera was perched on a down jacket. The jacket sat on a backpack. The backpack rested on a battered suitcase. He felt the rush of air as a five-year-old boy whizzed by just inches away, and in its wake, the shaky pile toppled to the floor in a heap. Luis shrugged as he continued to rearrange the money pack on his belt while fishing for his ID.

Checking in at a machine was easy, but it added a few steps to the task of getting your stuff to the plane's hold.

Still, there was something good about doing it yourself, doing anything yourself, really. When traveling, doing it yourself kept you thinking you might actually be in charge of something. So much of air travel was out of your control: the lines, the constantly changing schedules, and all the people that surround you. You put yourself in the hands of fate, Luis thought, and then you just got through it.

The little boy's mother rushed to restack the luggage, breathlessly apologizing for the energy of her small charge, but Luis waved her off. "Not a problem." He turned back to the machine.

All around him, dozens and dozens of people were starting their adventure.

Some were seasoned travelers, and some were new to the process.

"Reservation number? I don't have that. I wrote down the flight number, that's all."

"Down at the bottom, see? It asks how many bags you are going to check."

"Well of course, the dog counts as luggage."

"The nerve. My Annabelle is not luggage."

"Lady, it goes under the plane, in with the baggage, doesn't it?"

"And she is most definitely *not* an 'it!' Heavens!"

"Fifteen bucks? Each? Next thing you know, they'll charge you for sitting on the inside of the dang plane."

"This machine is not working. I'm

sure I pushed the right buttons. Can I talk to a person?"

"Checking two bags all the way to Pocatello, then?"

Luis had been traveling since he didn't know when. As a boy, he flew with his parents to visit family on both coasts a lot. Sometimes they went on vacation to foreign cities. They often went with Dad on business to countries as far away as Europe. More often, they accompanied him south of Luis' Texas home: Mexico, Guatemala, Costa Rica, Venezuela, Brazil.

In those days, he traveled in smarter clothes. He wore creased trousers and a sport jacket, a button down shirt and a tie that his mother fixed around his neck, standing behind him with his head resting against her waist. When the tie was just so, she would bend down to kiss the top of his head and declare the journey "will now commence. Master Luis is ready for flight."

Flying was an event in those days, and people dressed up. Stewardesses – that's what flight attendants were called – wore little hats, even in the plane, and gloves. If you were very good, or very lucky, or "so handsome, I could eat him," they pinned junior wings on your lapel. Whoever brought you to the aerodrome – that's what his father called it – waved you off from the ground below the mobile staircase that rolled up to the open door. It was so very different today. You were separated almost immediately by miles of corridors and glass.

His mother still confessed shock at the way people dressed to travel today, and her biggest complaint was leveled at passengers in shorts and flip-flops with baseball caps that stayed on heads the entire trip. Modern travelers drag all their belongings on to the plane to stuff in the tiny cabinets above their heads. In her day, luggage was whisked away by handlers, and she stepped on to a plane with a tiny purse, a hat pinned to her head, and a small boy's hand in hers. Like a princess, Luis used to think, or at least a movie star.

"Martha, I am not holding your purse while you take them to the bathroom. Can't she carry it? Makes a guy look like a dork."

"Careful of the wheels on that thing, Frances. You're running over your coat."

"Better that than his little brother."

"Depends."

"Now cut that out."

"You cut in that line, and security will be on you like ugly on an ape."

"April is such a better time. Less hassle. What possessed us to plan this month?"

"We've been over this a hundred times, Mike."

"Well, let's do a hundred and one. Really. Convince me."

Another small boy appeared in Luis' peripheral vision. Luis' eye caught the broadly striped shirt, and then he took in the copper hair standing on end. The child could not have been more than four or five years old, and he stared at Luis as though he knew him. Luis wondered, was this little guy lost? He scanned the crowd for a mother or a father, but when he turned back, the boy was gone.

"Mom, can I have the window? She always gets the window. Can I have the window? Can I, please?"

"Ask your father."

"Look at those clouds. I don't like the look of those clouds."

"Would you stop? There is nothing to worry about with those tiny little clouds. It's a gorgeous day!"

"Well, the clear days are the ones you have to worry about. They are just not safe for flying. Drafts and things. I saw it on TV."

"Cart on your right, people. Coming through. Cart on your right."

"You'll be just fine, dear."

"You're a good husband and a good father, but, Leonard, you do not know the first thing about aeronautics."

"Trust me, sweetheart, we will be fine. Statistics show that it is much safer than driving."

"Now he's an expert in statistics."

"Darling, if it's your time to go, you'll know it."

"Just because the pilot's number is up doesn't mean my number is up."

"Heavens."

TWO

Security

A tall, perfumed lady was pleading with the TSA guard.

"But I took out half of it and poured it down the sink."

"I am sorry, ma'am, but the bottle has to be smaller than three ounces."

"Do you have any idea how much that cost?"

"No, the socks can stay on, sir. Just the shoes."

"Female check on two. Repeat, female check on two."

"Run that bag through again, will you, Minnie? I think there might be a small dog in there. Collar's lighting up the machine."

"We've got time for coffee, if we ever get through this line."

"Whoa, watch where you're putting those hands, mister."

"Standard procedure now, sir. It's a pat down."

"You think I got a gun stashed in my pants?"

"Please remain calm, sir, and we'll have you on your way."

"I think my coat is stuck. Can you push it through?"

"What's with the x-ray? Is it radioactive?"

"And she said she was going to Zambia. I never heard of Zambia, did you?"

"Yeah, it's part of Australia. Or New Zealand, I forget which."

"No way. That would take forever."

A uniformed woman with more padding than patience was sorting a dozen shoes forgotten by a Cub Scout pack in over-full bins. The boys were skating with glee in their stocking feet on the slippery terminal floor.

"Incoming!"

"Take *that*, Dr Evil!"

"Ahhhhhhhhhhhh....ouch!"

The uniformed woman was going to have a hard time rounding them up.

"Get back here and claim these, fellas!"

Belt buckles, handfuls of coins, keys – the jangling sounds of people passing through metal detectors filled the air. Wheelchairs and baby carriages were searched separately and sent on. And lines and lines of travelers approached bored security guards like scolded puppies.

THREE

Security Breach

Luis recalled a trip his father made to France. He took Luis when he was just a little boy. Mother was not happy to see them go. Not happy at all. There had been explosions throughout the city of Paris: department stores, a post office, the police station, a bookstore, and then a shocking attempt on the Eiffel Tower. Luis remembered the "bee-baw, bee-baw" of police cars and a puff of smoke outside Tati's. It was so far away and so unreal that the boy thought it another adventure. He did not know about how many people had died until he was much older.

Standing in line at de Gaulle airport to come home, Luis and his father listened to the intercom. A very calm lady broadcast a message. Everyone was required to leave the terminal quickly but without panic. Guards had found an unattended case in one of the terminals and suspected the worst. Half an hour later, they were back in place, sort of in the same order, although some clever travelers had seized on the chance to move up in the line. It didn't really do them any good. The announcement was repeated, and everybody headed outside again.

Was it because the threat of attack was a new thing? Or was it because they were in France? There was just no panic. In fact, people were sort of jolly as they milled about the sidewalk outside the terminal. Luis remembered being cold, very cold. Dad chuckled at the smokers leaning against the building. "They aren't too worried, but then, if you consider those French cigarettes, these people have a death wish, don't they? Smell to high heaven. They don't call them 'galoshes' for nothing."

The drill happened many more times, and they moved in and out of the airport all morning long. After nearly half a dozen trips to the curb, they made their way to the gates and left faster than any boarding planes "in the history of the planet," Dad declared, "like greased lightning. I swear, if that blasted drill was called once more, the whole place would be shut down for days, baguettes, berets and all." Luis' eyes were big as saucers when the plane finally took off. He was excited by the danger, but didn't believe it had anything to do with him. He knew his father would protect him.

Then Luis grew up. He got a job, and he began to travel on his own. Photography became his life, and reporting on wars and civil unrest put him in some dicey situations. Dad wasn't around to protect him, but he had learned from this father to look straight at the world rather than glimpse it sideways with fear. So, he supposed Dad was still looking after him, in a way.

In his work, he had his share of boarding planes with guards, pointing to his bags on the tarmac before being let on board. He had been taken off one plane only to be bused to an identical plane further down the field. The idea was to throw off any chance of trouble. He had often mounted the stairs under the gaze of snipers or accompanied by soldiers with machine guns. Guns and soldiers came with the territory, and he took it in stride. Mostly, he didn't think about it.

But just now, he remembered being loaded onto his flight after a very drawn-out obstacle course in Turkey. Passengers were asked to take their seats according to their preference: smokers on the left, non-smokers on the right. He laughed that anyone thought that would work.

Sure, terrible things could happen, but most of the time, they just didn't.

FOUR

The Bad News

"For those passengers awaiting this flight, we have been instructed by ground control..."

A wave of groans filled the waiting area.

"Not that bad. Just a thirty-minute delay. We can still make our connection."

"Storms, do you think? That means it's going to be bumpy?"

"I'm going to get the kids some juice. You want water?"

"Sure, get it frozen and throw some booze on it."

"Harold, you untie that one more time, and I will make you wear those on your head."

"Please, the way to gate to Phoenix, please?"

"I'm going to try to charge my computer. Do you see any sockets?"

As the passengers rearranged themselves, Luis spied the boy in the striped shirt ambling toward the window. When the boy got close, he leaned into the glass, opened his little mouth into an "O" and breathed out. A foggy patch appeared on the pane. Very carefully, he began to draw images in the condensation. What were they? Houses? Luis watched as the boy's little finger filled every inch with a neighborhood. Just as carefully, the boy rubbed it away with his sleeve.

"Oh my God! I'm so sorry!"

Luis turned to see the result of a collision between the coffee cup of woman in a red suit and the bright white shirt of a man in jeans.

"Not to worry, little lady. I got another one."

"Soda water. Let me fetch you some soda water for that stain."

"Just go ahead and settle yourself down, ma'am. It ain't nothing."

"But it's hot! Are you burned?"

"Sugar, it ain't no hotter than a cool breeze. Don't you fret none."

And then the clean-up began. Luis turned back to watch the boy again, but found only an empty window, the trail of a little finger still in evidence.

"You put the tickets in your hat?"

"Sure, clever, huh? Nobody could steal them, and they are right with the toothbrushes."

"Please, to tell me where is Phoenix plane?"

Rustling caught Luis' attention. A thin, short family struggled with three small children and two older ones, maybe ten or eleven years old, twins. The sorry little group surely had come from far away. With all the cloth bags and plastic bags piled around them like a bunker, they looked exhausted. The baby looked out with sad eyes but didn't cry. Too tired, probably. Luis felt sorry for mom and dad with all those kids. They looked deflated, as if the air were leaked out of a tire. The announcement of further delay was not good news for them.

Luis looked up to the gate and wondered if they were on his flight. This was his gate. Over to the board, Luis confirmed that there was a delay, and then he checked his watch. Shouldn't be that big a deal. It was still morning, and he had all day to make it. He turned back to the young family, but they had been replaced by a flock of nuns.

Luis heard somebody say that life, in essence, was all about moving things from one place to another. That was it, the sum total. It used to be that it was stuff that got moved. Nowadays, it seemed people were the stuff that got moved from one place to another.

We are like little pellets, Luis thought, loaded into aircraft, like stones into slingshots, and fired into the sky.

Nobody went far from the gate during the thirty-minute delay. Since the time was so short, everyone was asked to "stay in the vicinity of the boarding lounge." An hour and fifteen minutes later, a queue started to form at the desk.

The podium, of course, was empty.

FIVE

Relocation Blues

"In Kiev, we have no such delay."

"I'm hungry, Boris. Do we have time to eat?"

"Bah, with first class meal on plane?"

"But the plane's not going anywhere."

"Americans have no patience. Come, little bird, to fill your beak."

The big-shouldered Russians led their women toward the food court.

What business brings them here, Luis wondered. How did they get here and how did they hook up with those Midwestern blondes?

Foreign service, missionary service, immigration, oil, gas, and now cell phones...there are so many reasons people ended up in a country not of their birth. The new global age made boundaries very thin. At least for some. Not everyone had such an easy time of it.

Some moves are bigger than others. Take that small family. Take any family, including Luis' own, that moved from one part of the world to another. "Relocation" they called it, and Luis had to get used to it early. He remembered with crystal clarity the feeling. Each time his family moved, he had to get used to a new house and find his new school. He was always adjusting to new friends and classmates. With his warm nature and his brave face, he quickly fit in with the other kids. But he never had a best friend, a friend he would keep from one move to another. There was never enough time, and you always had to be ready for the next move.

With a little smile on his face, Luis recalled his first crush at the ripe age of nine. Mirabelle had coal black hair that fell below her waist. He knew she liked him when she hauled off and punched him in the stomach as he tried to walk her home. It was a pulled punch; she hadn't hurt him much at all. That was the giveaway, and within a week, she relented. Years later, Luis could remember the pillowy softness of her lips when they practiced kissing under her grandmother's rickety stairs. "So we will learn how to get married," she said, and then wiped her mouth with the back of her hand. She was always practical, and she smelled like mango. He missed her terribly when his family moved in the middle of the school year.

Women were hard to live with, and they were hard to live without. Constantly being on the road made relationships a challenge for Luis. Still, he had to admit that he was often glad to see the next assignment come. A new shoot would let him get away from a new girl without guilt. He enjoyed his freedom, and, while he was not proud of it, he was sure he had broken a few hearts in his day. Only once did it catch up to him. That was Beatriz, who left him after a short but riotous affair in Montreal. Luis was not sure he would hurt like that again, and he tried to avoid it as best he could.

"For all passengers awaiting information on Flight 221, we have an update..."

WINGO PERSEUS

SIX

The Waiting Game

When it was called a ninety-minute delay, people started to move away from the gate. They moved to phones, to find food, to shop the newsstands, wandering the terminal to pass the time.

The families going long distances were getting harder to move. If anything, the space they occupied became larger and larger as gear neatly packed in bags got pulled out, used, and spread on chairs. It looked like they were leaking, and getting them whole again would take some work.

"Ben, I have some bad news. No way I am going to make the connection. Yes, I've tried them all....can we reschedule the cruise for January?"

"Hi, sweetheart. Been trying to get you. I miss you, too, but it won't be long now. How did your mother take it?"

"Take it out of the freezer, but put it in the fridge. You don't want it to thaw too fast. I could be a while."

"Long time ago, I used to go straight through but they canned the nonstop. Now I'm all over the country trying getting there. Leave it to my brother to live in God-forsaken Egypt."

"Well, tell them to bloody well move it! I can't fly the stupid plane myself! You want I should talk directly to Bob about this? Didn't think so. And get me a car, because I'm not going to try to get a cab at that hour...hey watch it!"

"Watch it yourself, pal."

"Who you calling 'pal?' No, not you, Barry, this guy who thinks he's the only person in the rotten airport."

"Well lookee who's talking. You got stock in luggage companies, buddy? Move it or lose it."

"You threatening me?"

"Nah, asking nicely. That's my foot under there, you know."

"You want to take it outside, big guy?"

"Sure, you head on out, and I'll meet you in a jiff."

Delays sure made folks hot under

the collar. The closest passengers, without making any eye contact, moved away from the scene. Not Luis. Luis watched it all.

SEVEN

Secure the Area

Luis watched it all. He didn't move. He'd seen that look in the eye before, and his mind wandered back to a shoot along the coast, very far away from here. A guy who knew a guy got Luis a meeting with a honcho in the resistance, and with strict orders to forget every inch of the way, which he couldn't see anyway on account of the blindfold, a meeting was arranged.

It became clear that the revolutionary liked to see his picture in the magazines, and Luis was selected for the honors.

His job was to get an exclusive shot of the boss on his own turf. He wanted to be pictured with a couple of his kids around him. The leader was trying to show that, contrary to official reports, the young people of his country were right behind his spotless intentions. That sort of thing. Luis would normally pass on the beauty shots, but the target had not been seen in more than a year, and many presumed him dead. A chance to take fresh photo was not to be missed by this photojournalist.

When the car arrived at its remote destination, Luis understood the only sound tolerated out of him was the click of the camera. Beer bottles and something stronger were passing among the men behind him.

"Here! Now!"

"He does not wait for *you!*"

With the sour taste of fear in his mouth, Luis was shoved forward with the barrel of a gun. It occurred him that to there were too many armed people dangerously close to wasted for this to go well. Somebody made a remark, and in a flash, guns were cocked. Luis heard the click of automatic weapons and a low murmur from the pumped-up foot soldiers. For what seemed like forever, two men stared at each other. When one cracked a smile, the tension eased, at least enough for them to walk away from the situation. He memorized the sound of the surf, the faint waft of pot, a gleam in somebody's eye, all tropical and idyllic, and all screwed up.

With a break in the action, Luis was bundled back into the beaten Ford, head under the seat, and raced back toward town. He lost a couple rolls of films and a very expensive lens. He lost his nerve, too, and had to force himself to walk, not crawl, away from the car when his drivers saw fit to release him. But he had the shot.

Back in the cabana, he began to breathe again. The "resort" was not much more than a timber pyramid with a big room downstairs and a sleeping loft above it. All of the space was open to the elements. He lay back on the cot and let the gentle drift of sawdust fall on his face as termites bored into the logs above his head. After a little, then a lot of tequila with his jovial host, he found a calm center. Hearing the ocean throb in the background, he fell into a sleep as deep and untroubled as he had ever experienced in his life. He understood that life can go from dull to terrifying and back to dull as quick as that. His dad said life was like being an airplane pilot hours of boredom interrupted by a few minutes of pure terror.

And it was the terror, the adrenaline he found himself looking for more often than not. He wondered what others did for that kind of juice.

WINGO PERSEUS

EIGHT

Time Passes

Waiting is a learned art, Luis reflected. As a seasoned traveler, he was, he thought, pretty good at it. He had his books and his iPad to keep himself busy. He practiced patience and didn't get mad.

"We're going to stay right here in case they take off. Just like the blighters to leave without us."

"Oh, man, I could have stayed in bed another twenty minutes."

"Serves you right for coming in at two in the morning."

"But what a gig! Who gets to see Red Meat open? Awesome!"

"Sure, but lose the shades. You look like a drug dealer."

"Not with this head, man."

The sunglasses stayed on.

"Head for the car rental as soon as we get there. I'll pick up the bags."

"They can't really start without us, can they?"

"No telling with that bunch of animals."

"They will take all the pets out of the hold, won't they? I hate to think of Annabelle in the dark all this time."

"Nah, they'll keep her inside the terminal until we're cleared. They won't load anything until we go, in case they have to change planes."

"Change for Chicago, maybe? See if we can drive from there?"

"Oh, have a little patience."

But patience was in short supply.

Except for a young couple in the corner. They had multiple wires coming out of their heads and hands – iPods, cell phones, and they were all tangled in a heap. But the couple was as sound asleep as two babies in their cribs, her hand curled over the top of his head. They looked interwoven, their foreheads touching. He snored just a little. Luis closed his eyes. He remembered.

WINGO PERSEUS

NINE

Time, and Time Again

He knew a girl when she was very young, now that he stopped to think about it. Maybe nineteen or twenty; he was never exactly sure. Back then, he was shooting for a news story on the fledgling peace in the North of Ireland, and she was an occasional student in Queens. With Luis' leather jacket and the bag of film and his look of experience, she, of course, fell for him, hard. But so young, she was so young. She really was a beautiful kid beneath the attitude and the mouth and the wild hair. She behaved like a young James Dean in drag, all the moves of a village poet. But so damn young.

Their affair was tender, and she was a little stiff until a trip abroad loosened her inhibitions. Then it was time for the next assignment. For some reason, he had delayed taking a new story longer than usual; he was getting comfortable. But he had to work eventually. To his dismay, she was awfully clingy. The tough act dissolved, and he found himself with a hassle. He began to wipe her out of his mind. After all, she was a child, a pain, a nuisance. It was years later when he remembered her face looking out over the sea, her life in front of her, that he missed the smell of her skin. And that way she brushed the hair up off of her face, like a child intent on a sidewalk game.

In their most private moments, when it was quiet and the night was very late, he would look down at her. She seemed small in contrast to her big-ass attitude. She was so pale that she glowed in the firelight of the flat that was their only refuge. He made sure she hit the road before the landlady caught a whiff and sent her out into the night to her own rooms at sometimes two—sometimes three, even—in the morning. She was so eager, he figured he was doing her a favor. She was so eager, maybe she was doing him a favor.

It was a northern winter evening. The sun had set near three in the afternoon. She had gone down the country to visit a roommate's family and to see what the Irish called the Troubles up close. He had been close enough, thank you very much, and the excitement of soldiers was lost on him. A little out of character, he collected her at the station. When she stepped off the train, it was all he could do to resist running toward her, and he surprised himself. Instead he put a hand out to help her down and kissed her on the mouth, a kiss so soft and so young and so fresh that he thought he was tasting the beginning of time.

He supposed she knew more than her years but in all, he had to move on.

She was still just a silly girl of twenty. There was the world to see. She had the rest of college, he had the rest of his life, and their parting was amicable. He wasn't sure she knew it was final. A few letters trickled in then stopped. She got finally got it.

Last year he saw her again. He was flying through the city he remembered she fancied, and he looked her up out of curiosity. And there she was in the book.

She had finished school and had a few experiences under her belt. She had lived abroad, had gone to work and had got a little older, like everybody else.

They had dinner in a hotel, which was safe and neutral. He was curious, happy and a little excited to see her. They talked about most things, moved toward certain subjects and away from others. They were having a good time. Feeling a little sentimental, he casually said he thought he had room in his life now to see her once in a while. He moved around so very much but occasionally he was in town, and maybe they could start something, you know, without any strings.

She reached across the table and took his right hand in hers. It startled him but he was hooked. He let it rest. She held his hand in hers for a long time while he remembered a family ring she always wore on that hand. Where was it? And he thought how small her wrist was.

She turned his over, as if to study his palm, and then turned it back again. She looked into his eyes and slowly placed his hand back on the table. Just before the entrées arrived, she stood up and headed toward the restroom. He waited until the food was cold to inquire of the waiter if he had seen the girl. Was she on the phone?

"She left some time ago."

"Left? The building?"

"Yes, sir."

"Really? Did she say where she was going?"

"No, sir."

"Did she say anything at all?"

"Yes, sir."

"Well?"

"I asked her what I should tell her

dinner companion."

"And?"

"She said, 'Anything you like,' sir. 'Anything you like.'"

Luis did not see it coming. He never expected she would not sign on for the affair. She had grown up when he was not looking.

Thinking of that night, he knew that he had kept himself remote for too long. He felt like a person looking out of a plane at the world, thousands and thousands of feet below.

Of course, he made sure he always was.

TEN

Uniforms

"....announcing Flight 47. At this time, we'd like to invite members of our armed services to board at this time."

Lucky sods, thought Luis. Their flight's on time. When he looked at the four young men with pink shaved heads and camouflage fatigues, he had to reevaluate his position on that. Luck was something those boys required, and big time. From the shine on their faces and the youth in their eyes, it was clear they were not very long in the service. That plane was probably not taking them anywhere good.

"Yo, man. Switch with me. Get me away from that window."

"All going the same place, brother."

"Can't stand flying."

"You telling me this now? You know how far we gotta go in one of these contraptions?"

"Contrary to your belief, young man, airplane flight is immensely safer than any other mode of transport. And thank you, son, for your service."

"He's right, man. Plane's a hell of a lot safer than humvees. Or civilian traffic, for that matter. Or on the freeway with twenty women drivers or something."

"Watch it, Private." The woman's

lapels spoke volumes. "You could be depending on females who don't take too kindly to the insult."

"Ma'am, yes, ma'am. Sorry, ma'am. Just having a little fun."

"And you can get that out of your mind, too," she tossed over her shoulder as she marched onto the jetway.

"You'll be fine, man. Plane's as safe as your momma's arms."

"Yeah, it's the damn destination that kills you."

Nervous laughter.

"Bring on the humvees."

"Man, you couldn't find the front end of a hummer, much less drive it. Get going."

"Drives me crazy, this cell phone. Now I got three messages, and they are all from yesterday."

"You're going to get a tumor with those things in your ears."

"Ears and nose and toes. You try."

"Eees 'n' ohs 'n' toes!"

"That's right! Such a big girl!"

Giddy laughter.

As the baby made contact with the burliest of recruits a swift blue bunny to the back of the head the men jumped. A tense moment ensued until the GI bent down to retrieve the toy. Handing it back to the mother, he paused to touch the little girl on her chin.

"Keepin' me on my toes, right, little darlin'?"

The baby squealed, giggled and lobbed it again.

"Now welcoming our first class passengers. Passengers seated in rows one and two may board at this time."

Lucky sods.

WINGO PERSEUS

ELEVEN

Time Stops

"Weather."

"Crew change."

"Labor action."

Throughout the airport, passengers were confronted with the entire list of reasons for flight delay, Luis had heard them all before.

"Mechanical."

At the sound of mechanical problems, Luis laughed, thinking about the planes he had flown. Many of them should never have left the ground, and yet here he stood, no worse for wear.

"Lawn dart," that's what his fellow passenger—one of four that fit—called the twin engine heap that carried him from one island to another in the Pacific. He saw glimmers of the sea below through cracks in the floorboards.

"Not a confidence builder, is it, buddy? Your insurance up to date?"

"Tree Top Airline." That's what another passenger called the military transport that carried him to a shoot outside Kabul. Luis was not quite sure what crop—or product—or weapon made the lumps in that canvas mound, but he sat on it as they bounced over the arid landscape.

No pretzels or orange juice on those flights. The idea of a flight attendant was a luxury, in his mind. He only had that kind of service when he was flying domestic jumps. Where were the flight attendants on this flight, by the way? Were they stuck on a beached plane?

No, Luis realized. The flight attendants had given up long ago and headed for coffee. How often do they plan on sleeping in one city and end up hundreds of miles away? It comes with the job, Luis thought. What a way to make a living. Maybe that accounts for their steel in dealing with passengers. Luis would never cross them. Not on your life.

Sometimes, he thought, the work was pretty exotic. Heading to an assignment in Brazil years ago, he watched, amazed, when the attendants came off shift. Sure, it was a long flight. But just clock out? The flight attendants, all women, all young and beautiful, had boarded the plane long before the passengers for a four a.m. flight to the interior. At some signal, one by one, they entered the first class lavatory in uniform and emerged fifteen minutes later in very civilian high heels, tight skirts and mounds of eyelashes. Then, they simply sat down in open seats. In-flight service ended on the spot. When the plane landed, passengers saw themselves off the plane and wished themselves a happy onward journey.

Across the terminal, at a gate on the other side of the aisle, Luis saw another group of travelers dealing with a delay. In the middle sat an older couple. She read her magazine. He sat quietly in his own thoughts. They looked awfully patient, and what was that on her jacket? A pin of some sort. He tried to make it out.

"Passengers on Flight 221. We will have an update for you at the top of the hour. We apologize for the inconvenience and are doing everything we can..."

Why can't they tell you up front so you can sleep a little longer or drive, for goodness sake? The phone was running low and the book was boring. What was it that made him buy biographies of people he's supposed to care about rather than a good novel or a piece of fluff for that matter. Rove was making him ill.

He was tired. He sat down, and he looked around. He pulled the speakers out of his ears and heard the din of hundreds, maybe thousands of people, milling and breathing, walking, running, looking at the board, each one with a different destination, a different story.

Luis, lost in his thoughts, started to steam up. Settle down, he told himself. You've lasted longer.

And he imagines the open air on the other side of these windows. People are amassed here inside this steel and glass barn. Outside, they are driving their cars, going to the grocery store, walking the dog, making love, making money, living their lives.

In his daydream, he is busting out of the airport, jumping into a fast car. It's a yellow convertible, and he is roaring down the road, up to the mountains. No, better still, he's heading out to the coast. Yes, that's right, up Route One on the vast coast of California, past the low shore with birds...where is that place?...past the whales rounding Point Reyes and up into the hills above Bodega Bay that remind him so much of Ireland.

He can even see the cows, black as coal against the Sonoma clover. And the sandbar where the ocean meets the Russian River at Jenner, where harbor seals bask in the sun. And he senses that anything is possible in the quiet, in the green, with the wide Pacific shining so bright that it makes him squint. And he can smell the ocean and hear it crash. There's a faint mist from the surf pounding the rocks and flying up over the headland.

He can hear the tattlers on the rocks.

"Threet, threet, threet, threet, threet"

"You think we'll board today?"

And the yellowlegs' little hoot, and the sorrowful call of the osprey. He hears the chatter of the seashore.

"I say, you expect we're going anytime soon?"

He realizes he's hearing a human voice among the shorebirds.

With a pop in his ears, the bubble

broke. Luis was surprised to see a young woman in front of him. He was counting the row of rings up her left ear lobe and trying to identify the kind of bird that was tattooed on her shoulder. It was so tiny and hard to make out, but the overall impression was fine, like Japanese art.

"Sorry, man."

With a start, Luis realized this vision was talking to him. Right at him.

"Oh, what? Er? Well, I don't work for the airlines."

"Well, that ticket in your pocket already gave you away. Just thought you looked like somebody who, you know, does this a lot. Didn't mean to bother you." And she began to walk away.

"No, no no!" he roared, way too loudly. "You didn't bother me. I was thinking about something...else...and I didn't hear you."

He was digging himself in deeper, but she just smiled. A small smile. A tired smile.

"Going home?"

"Sure wish I was. I'm off to an audition, and I'm not going to get it. Waste of money. And now I'm not going to get there at all."

"If they cancel, you can get your money back."

"Well, that's good news. See, I knew you knew stuff."

TWELVE

Ready to Go

Hours had passed. The sun had set ages ago. He saw the same little striped boy being led down a long corridor, hand in hand with a woman in airline uniform. He was licking a white ice cream cone and walked with purpose. Most of his treat was on his shirt, making music out of his stripes. And yet, he looked dignified and sure. Luis wondered where his people were, if he had any. The boy gave a long, lingering look over his shoulder at Luis as he receded.

"Ladies and Gentlemen, Flight 1219 has been canceled, so this is the only plane out of here tonight. We cannot accommodate all the passengers who would like to travel, so we are looking for volunteers. You can earn a $250 travel coupon for your seat. If your travel plans are flexible, please see the agent at Gate Ten. Again, we do not have enough seats to accommodate...."

"Oh, man, I could use the money. Want to go tomorrow?"

"They don't give you money, just a ticket on another flight that will probably get delayed, too."

"I'm not sleeping on a bench!"

"What do you think, Mary? Should we call the kids?"

"Means this flight is really going

this time, so I am hanging on to my ticket, and so are you."

Chatter and bargaining filled the lounge. Will we? Won't we?

"Can they make you get off?"

"Like to see them try. My brother's a lawyer."

"Your brother flunked the bar three times. Take the money."

A few souls went to the counter and surrendered their tickets. The rest of the weary passengers could see them heading for the main terminal clutching dinner vouchers in their hands. It still seemed a pretty full departure lounge to Luis. All these people on just one plane?

Luis' new companion leaned toward him. As she brushed the hair from her face, he saw the amber flecks in her green eyes. She came in close, and he smelled rose water.

"I think they have a big old coin, and we'll all flip to see who gets on."

"Pretty arbitrary, don't you think? I am sure they have a better system."

"What's arbitrary about it? It all comes down to fate in the end."

"You believe that? Everything is destined?"

"Well, who's to say it isn't? What chain of events that took all day! I might add has us sitting here chatting? Don't you feel like we were on a course for this day?"

"Now you're spooking me," Luis laughed. "Like there is something strange going on with our plane. Are we going into a time warp, like they do in a sci-fi movie? I think it's just a matter of course. Happens all the time."

"Nah, not the plane. With us. It might happen all the time, but right now, right here, it is happening to us. Seems like fate to me."

"Well then fate is proximity—it's just who you end up next to."

"Exactly!" the girl beamed and tossed back her hair. "Now you're catching on!"

"I have to say it's okay ending up next to you; I am enjoying your... perspective. But as to fate, then all these people were fated to meet today."

"You catch on fast."

"So there's really nothing special

about it. Or weird. Or strange. Fate is just what happens."

"Except to us. You and me. Doesn't it feel like we've known each other all along?"

Luis had to admit she was right.

"For those passengers waiting on Flight 221, we are now heavily oversold. We are looking for volunteers to go on the next flight in the morning. If you are willing to give up your seat, you will earn a travel voucher for five hundred dollars and we will put you up in the airport hotel. Travel vouchers have no black-out dates and can be used for domestic as well as international travel. Again, we are looking for volunteers...."

That's the fate we sign on for in the skies, Luis thought. In life, people come together and move apart, like vast seas ruled by tides. It's astonishing to think how random it all is, but giving up control puts one in unusual situations. They were along for the ride, that was certain.

And what about this strange young woman? Luis wondered at her calm, her certainty, at the same time he suspected she was slightly off her rocker. Well, in a good way, anyway. Seeing the world fresh.

They talked, they debated, they sat in silence. At one point, when she was focused on texting from her phone, he looked over at a face that brought back a memory of a time lost, an age ago.

She tossed her hair. She yawned. She fell asleep.

Across the aisle, Luis' eyes settled on the older couple again. Their delay had lengthened as well. Yet, in the midst of the chaos, they sat like royalty, husband and wife. She wore a lilac jacket. Her nearly-white hair was set just so, and her sparkling eyes, sweet yet tired, looked out of gold-framed glasses. Beside her, her husband of many years wore a baby-blue sport coat, white shirt and tie. From their perfect grooming to their white hair to their pale faces to their spotless demeanor, they spoke of another time. So different, they were, from the black- and grey- clothed youth surrounding them.

An airline bag from a carrier that no longer flew sat at her heels. Quietly, without disturbing anything in the air, they breathed in the commotion around them. The old man had been to the counter earlier in the hour and, satisfied with the information he got, sat back down with a sigh to wait, two boarding passes in his breast pocket.

People came. They went. Still, the couple sat, watching, as though fifty years provided a vantage point, a private balcony for them to see the world's workings.

There was a little flurry of activity when and airline person stepped to the counter and announced boarding. The woman popped up like a lawn sprinkler as he said to her, "Come on,

Ma. Get your hat on, we're going." He took her hand, and they walked down the jetway. Luis could see, now that she had turned, that it was a butterfly pin on her lapel. They emanated the soft pastel light of old age.

"You see them, too," said the tattooed girl. "They are lovely, aren't they? I've been watching them and wondering, what's their story? Were they like that from the moment they met, or just because of all those years together? Is that fate? What do they make of all this? What makes them so calm? They don't seem to be flapped at all. But then, they've practiced waiting a lot longer than we have."

"For those passengers on Flight 221, we are looking for just two more seats.

If your travel plans are flexible..."

Luis looked at the girl and smiled.

"My name is Clara," she said.

WINGO PERSEUS

THIRTEEN

Landing

The sun came through the windows like a blaze of light.

It was a quiet morning in the airport, midweek, routine flights, clear skies and smooth sailing. Passengers moved about with ease, smiling at each other, helping people with their bags. It was a day that made folks want to fly. The world was fresh and young.

"Flight 221 is now accepting all passengers, all rows. Please limit your carry-on to…"

A little boy ran to the window to see the plane. On his lapel, he wore a pair of wings his dad got from an airline that didn't even exist anymore. Still, the boy wore his pin with pride.

"Grandma will be so surprised, right, Momma?"

"Yes, dear...and you look so handsome in your sport coat."

"She let me help with cookies last time. I put candy for eyes. Remember?"

"Of course, I do, darling. You are her Favorite Boy."

"And Grandpa and I make Big Plans for town. Maybe he'll let me drive!"

"Soon, love, very soon."

"And here, Momma? Was it here you knew?"

"Yes, child, right in this airport. I knew your father was the one. It was fate."

"Do you have the tickets, love?" He saw the sun glint off gold along her left ear. An ear he never tired of kissing.

"Tickets and toddler, all accounted for."

"Then shall we see what fate holds next for us?"

At the last moment, she slips her tattooed arm into his as Luis takes the boy's hand. They step into the jetway, together.